To Mary —
Happy Halloween!
William F. Boyd

ACKNOWLEDGEMENTS:

Many thanks to our consultants:
Nancy Mays & children:
Liam....age 4
Chris....age 6
Cheryl..age 7
Tim......age 8

AUTHOR'S DEDICATION:

To all who joined with me in the
quest to rediscover some of the lost
innocence of Halloween:
Mimi, Bill Jr., Janice, Madeline, Ross,
Theresa, David, Benjamin, Lindsay,
Ross Jr., Michael, and other fellow
enthusiasts Mary Jo, Mary Lou and Tracy.

ILLUSTRATOR'S DEDICATION:

To my sweet pumpkins, Emily and Elliot.

Wyatt Press, 15005 W. 167th Terrace, Olathe, KS 66062

ISBN 0-9718161-0-7

LCCN 2002101818

Wyatt Press First Edition

Printed in USA by Walsworth Publishing

The Pumpkin Fairy

Written by
William T. Boyd

Illustrated by
Mary Jo Roberts

Once upon a Halloween, a new little fairy sat shivering on a pumpkin shell. Like all new fairies, she had to find the right good deed to earn her magic powers. But by nightfall, try as she might, she hadn't found the right good deed, or even a warm place to stay. All the hollow trees were full of owls and other creatures, and the torn and threadbare clothes of Tatterpatches, the friendly scarecrow, couldn't protect her from the frosty cold.

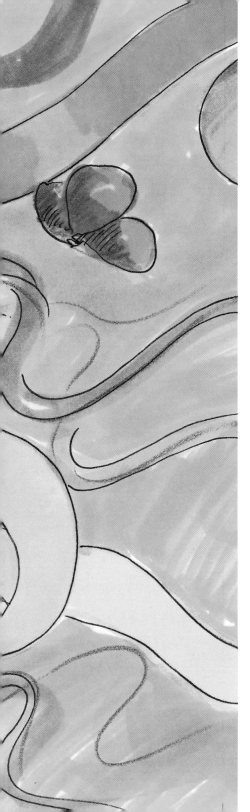

"Oh, woe is me!" she sighed, feeling very sorry for herself. Suddenly, a deep, mellow voice that echoed as if it came from a cave said: "You are welcome to stay in my shell." The fairy jumped straight up in the air. As she floated back down, she exclaimed to the pumpkin, "You can talk!"

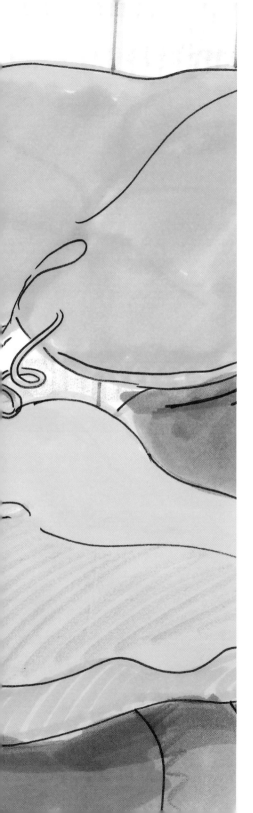

"Yes," came the calm reply. "My name is Rollo, Rollo Pumpkin. I think you'll find my shell quite comfortable." "Oh, I'm so pleased," cried the fairy. "What can I give you in return for your kindness?" "Well," Rollo said sadly, "the only thing we pumpkins wish for are funny, scary faces, but since the farmer didn't take us to market, the children won't be able to give them to us in time for Halloween."

"Oh, I can fix that," the fairy said happily. "When I get my magic powers, I will grant you and all your friends your wish!" Delighted, Rollo rocked to and fro, and all the other pumpkins bounced up and down, shaking their leaves with excitement.

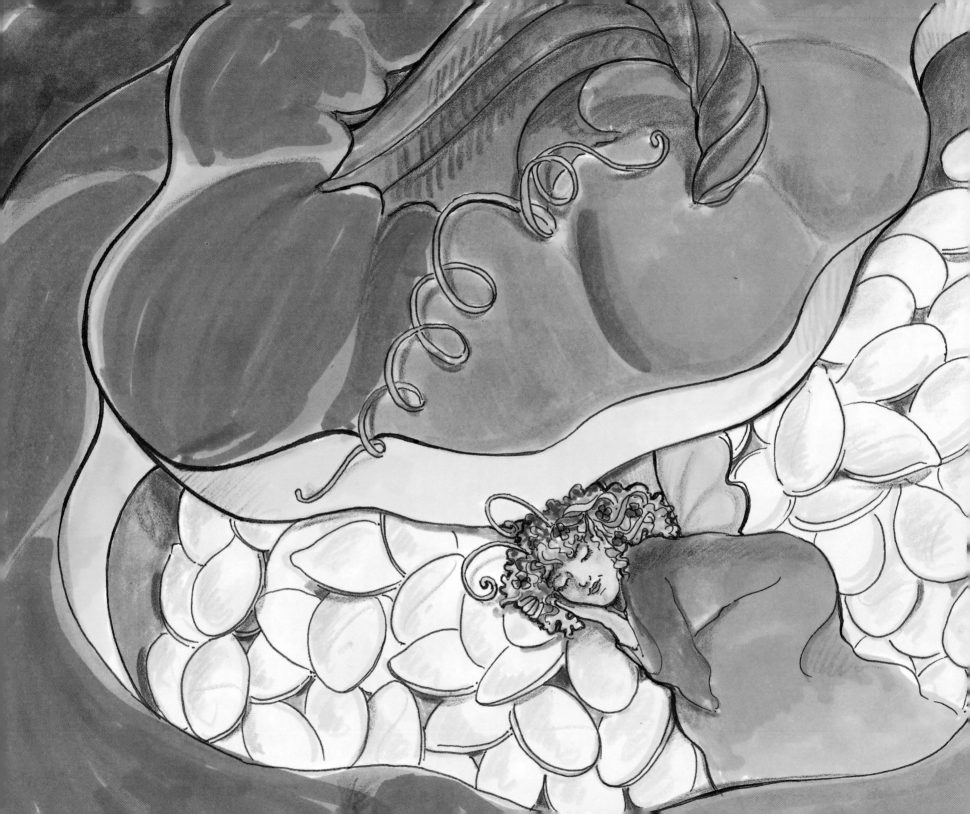

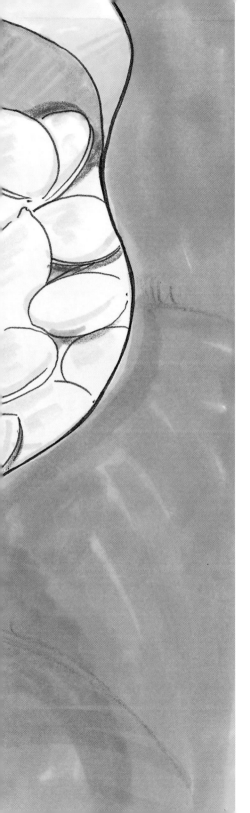

Just as Rollo promised, the fairy found his shell to be wonderfully warm and snug. She had never been so cozy as she nestled down among the fluffy pumpkin seeds. She was just nodding off to sleep when she heard a great fuss. Rollo was trembling and all his neighbors were crying for help.

Over the din she could hear a loud, raspy voice shouting: "Grab'em boys. There's nothing better than fat, juicy pumpkins!" She knew that voice. It belonged to Roggar, leader of the coyote pack. She was very upset because she hadn't earned her magic powers in time to help her new friends. Tatterpatches, the scarecrow, had done his very best to stop the coyotes but, after all, scarecrows can only jiggle and shake. The coyotes were grabbing pumpkins right and left.

The fairy knew something had to be done
and done quickly. Suddenly, she remembered
the pumpkins' wish and knew what had to be
done. In a twinkling, she flew up above the
pumpkin patch and sang this magic chant:
"Pumpkin hearts I give a flame to,
jack-o-lanterns now I name you."

At that command the patch grew bright
from the light of a hundred shining faces,
and caught Roggar in middle flight, leaping
for a pumpkin. He plopped down on
something that used to be a pumpkin but
it wasn't a pumpkin anymore!

He and his gang were surrounded by dreadful frights, with flashing eyes and laughing mouths big enough to swallow them up! More frightened than they had ever been in their lives, the coyotes scrambled through the clinging vines and scurried off into the darkness, never to be seen again.

As their howls faded away in the distance, a peaceful quiet settled over the pumpkin patch. The happy glow from each smiling face told the fairy she had truly found the right good deed for her magic powers. The pumpkin patch would be her home and she would be known forever after as the Pumpkin Fairy, friend of the pumpkins and guardian of the pumpkin patch.

And she can be seen today, flitting and darting like a firefly among the pumpkin vines, by anyone who believes in the magic of Halloween.